HENRY
AND THE
YETI

BLOOMSBURY
LONDON OXFORD NEW YORK NEW DELHI SYDNEY

A RUSSELL AYTO PRODUCTION

For my mother and father

Bloomsbury Publishing,
London, Oxford, New York, New Delhi and Sydney

First published in Great Britain in 2017 by Bloomsbury Publishing Plc
50 Bedford Square, London WC1B 3DP

www.bloomsbury.com

BLOOMSBURY is a registered trademark of Bloomsbury Publishing Plc

Text and illustrations copyright © Russell Ayto 2017

The moral rights of the author/illustrator has been asserted

A CIP catalogue record of this book is available from the British Library

ISBN 978 1 4088 7660 2 (HB)   ISBN 978 1 4088 7661 9 (PB)   ISBN 978 1 4088 8282 5 (eBook)

All papers used by Bloomsbury Publishing are natural, recyclable products made from wood grown in well managed forests.
The manufacturing processes conform to the environmental regulations of the country of origin

Printed in China by Leo Paper Products, Heshan, Guangdong

1 3 5 7 9 10 8 6 4 2

Henry loves yetis.
Yes, *yetis*.

Yet nobody knows if yetis actually exist.

"Yetis?" says Henry's father. "Hmm, nobody actually knows."

But Henry is sure yetis do exist . . .

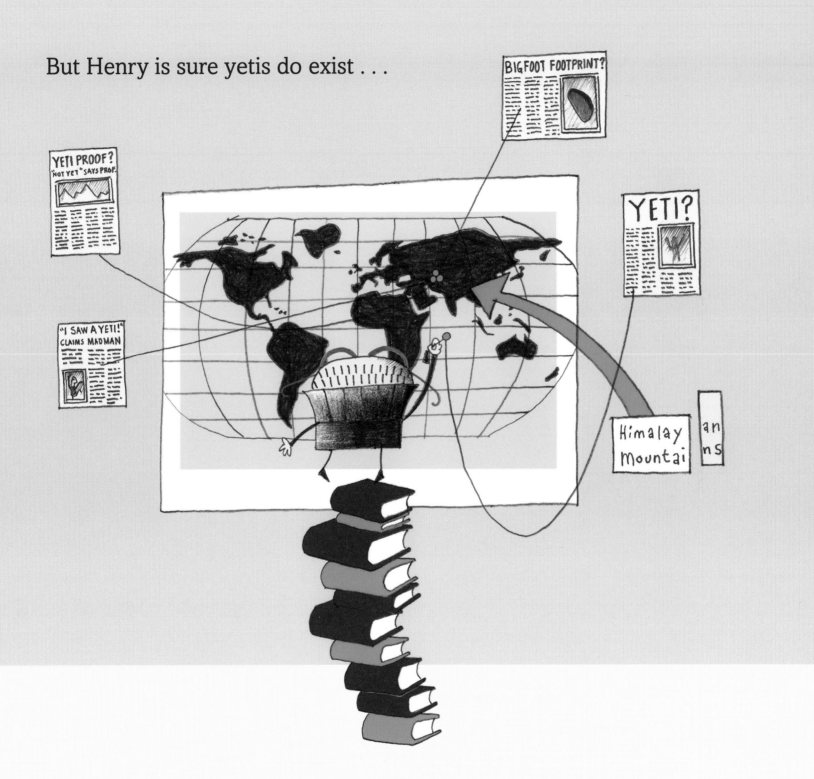

so he will go on an expedition to find one.

Henry asks his headteacher if he
can miss school to go on the expedition.

"Yetis?" says
the headteacher.
"They don't exist."

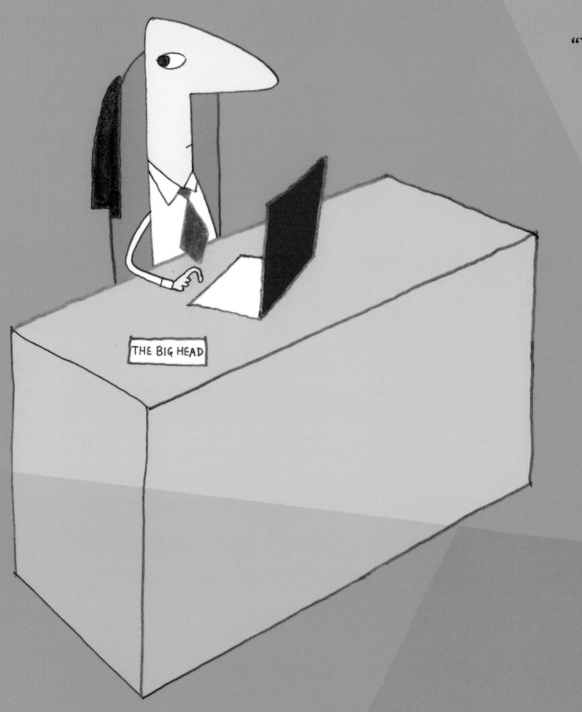

THE BIG HEAD

"This is a school announcement. Henry is going on an expedition to find a yeti!"

Everybody laughs.

Ha ha ha! Ha ha ha!

"And if you do happen to see one," says the headteacher, "don't forget to bring back some evidence."

Henry packs all the equipment
he needs for the expedition.

A waterproof
hammock.

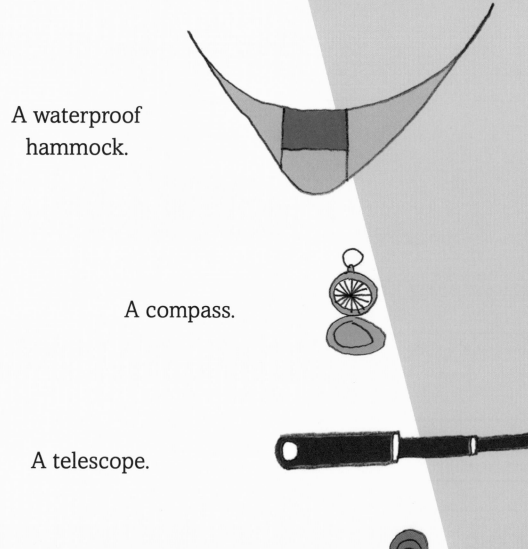

A compass.

A telescope.

A climbing rope.

And a camera to take pictures for evidence.

Now Henry is ready.

"Remember, **no** staying
up late," says Henry's father.

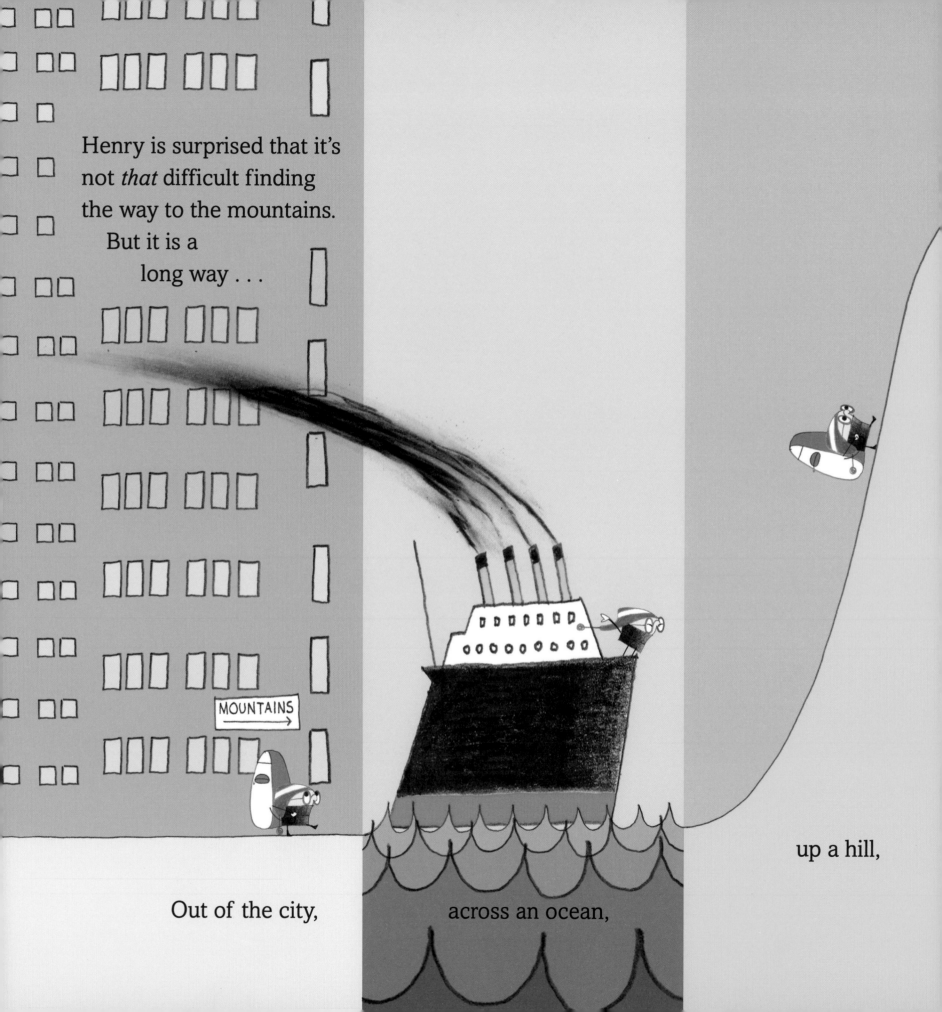

Henry is surprised that it's
not *that* difficult finding
the way to the mountains.
But it is a
long way . . .

MOUNTAINS →

Out of the city,

across an ocean,

up a hill,

over a river,

and through a dense forest
(all without staying up late),

until . . .

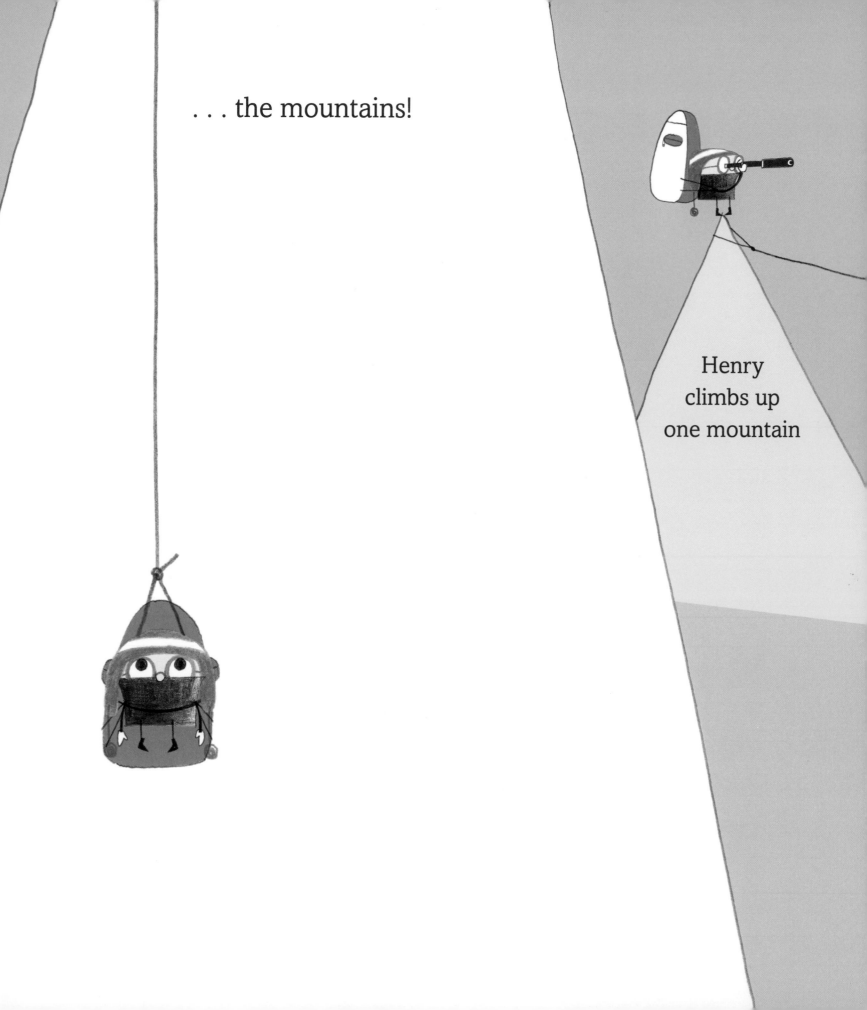

. . . the mountains!

Henry
climbs up
one mountain

after another,

searching **everywhere** for a yeti.

But Henry finds nothing.
There is no sign of a yeti anywhere.
Not even a suspicious-looking footprint.

Henry was sure yetis do exist,
but now he isn't so sure.

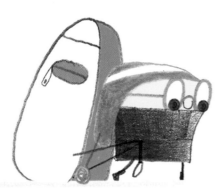

Maybe he should just turn around and go right back . . .

Oh!

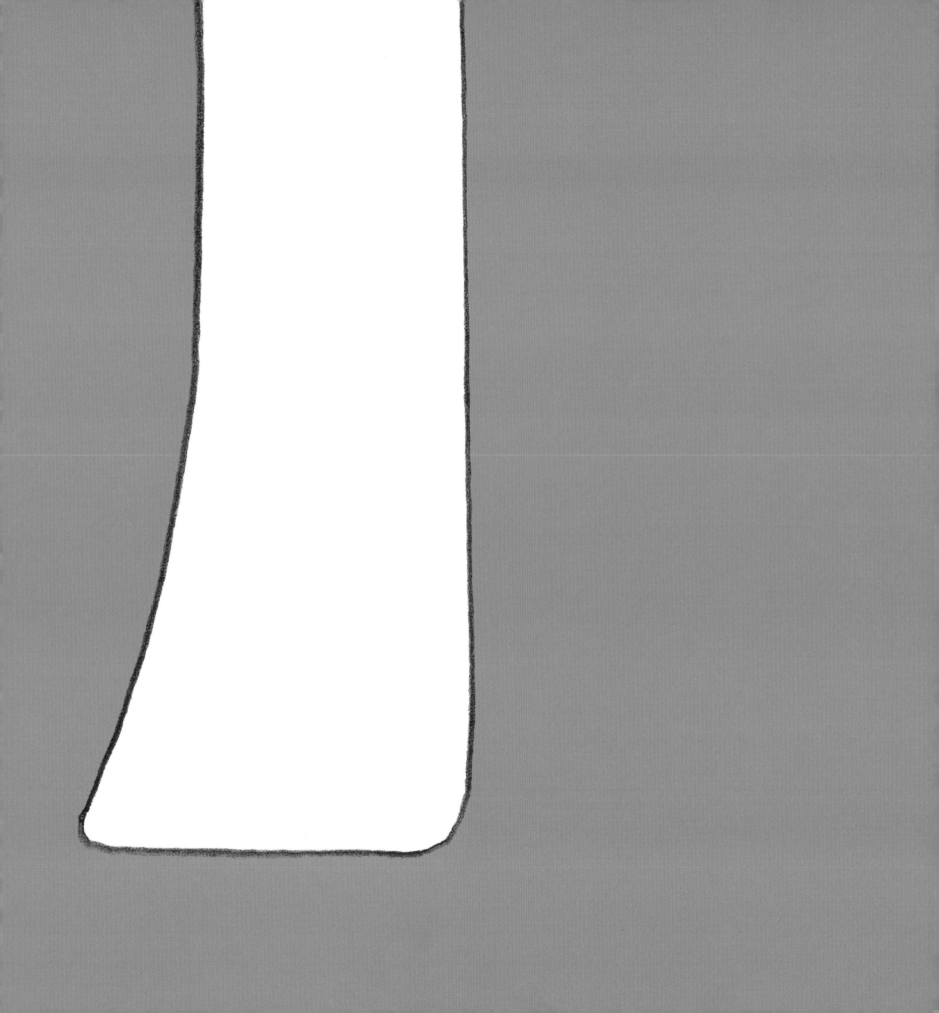

Henry sees a yeti.
The yeti sees Henry.

The yeti is slightly **bigger** than Henry expects.
And more friendly.

Henry takes pictures of
the yeti for evidence.

Then they
play hide and seek.

Now it is time for Henry to go home.

Henry is surprised that it's more
    difficult knowing the way back . . .

MOUNTAINS

so he uses his compass to find the right way home.

"Well?" says Henry's father.

"I didn't stay up late once," says Henry.

"No," says Henry's father. "Did you see a yeti?"

"Oh yes!" says Henry. "Yetis do exist! And I've brought back the evidence."

Henry unpacks all the equipment.

A climbing rope.

A telescope.

A compass.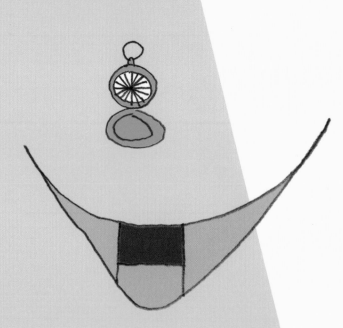

And a waterproof
hammock.

Wait a minute!
No camera.

"No camera!"
says Henry.

"No camera, no evidence," says Henry's father.

"No evidence," says Henry.

"No evidence!" says the headteacher.

"Write me ten million lines for making things up. Yetis indeed!"

Everybody laughs.

million lines! 10 million lines! 10 million line
million lines! 10 million lines! 10 million line
million lines! 10 million lines! 10 million line
million lines! 10 million lines! 10 million line
million lines! 10 million lines! 10 million line
million lines! 10 million lines! 10 million line
million lines! 10 million lines! 10 million line
million lines! 10 million lines! 10 million line
million lines! 10 million lines! 10 million line
million lines! 10 million lines! 10 million line
million lines! 10 million lines! 10 million line
million lines! 10 million es! 10 million line
million lines! 10 m es! 10 million line
million lines! 10 m es! 10 million line

What can Henry do now?
He is **not** making things up. He **did** see a yeti. Yetis **do** exist.

But nobody, except his own father, believes him.

Oh!
Henry sees the yeti again.

The yeti sees Henry.
The headteacher sees the yeti.

And everybody stops laughing.

Now the headteacher is
having a lie down.

The yeti gives Henry back his camera.

Henry is thinking he will probably not have to write ten million lines after all.

Henry loves yetis.
Yes, *yetis.*

THE END